M.K.

HAWKEYE COLLINS & AMY ADAMS in

THE SECRET OF THE
LOON LAKE MONSTER

& OTHER MYSTERIES

by M. MASTERS

D0167239

Meadowbrook Books
18318 Minnetonka Blvd.
Deephaven, MN 55391

This book is dedicated to all the children across the country who helped us develop the *Can You Solve the Mystery?* ™ series.

Library of Congress Cataloging in Publication Data

Masters, M.
Hawkeye Collins & Amy Adams in The secret of the Loon Lake monster & other mysteries.

(Can you solve the mystery?; v. 10) Summary: Two twelve-year-old sleuths solve a series of mysteries using sketches of important clues.
[1. Mystery and detective stories] I. Title. II. Title: Hawkeye Collins and Amy Adams in The secret of the Loon Lake monster.   III. Title: Loon Lake monster. IV. Series: Masters, M. Can you solve the mystery?; v. 10.
PZ7.M42392Hkc   1984   [Fic]   83-23676

ISBN 0-88166-050-7 (paperback)

10 9 8 7 6 5 4 3 2 1
Printed in the United States of America.

Copyright ©1984 by Meadowbrook Creations.

"The Secret of the Loon Lake Monster"
by Jean Nugent and Katy Brown.
All other stories by Deborah Felder.
Editorial services by Parachute Press, Inc.
Illustrations by Brett Gadbois.
Cover art by Robert Sauber.

CONTENTS

READ THE SOLUTIONS IN YOUR MIRROR

Would you like to become a member of the CYSTM?™ Reading Panel? See details on page 95.

Amy Adams

Hawkeye Collins

Young Sleuths Detect Fun in Mysteries

By Alice Cory
Staff Writer

Lakewood Hills has two new super sleuths watching over its citizens. They are Christopher "Hawkeye" Collins and Amy Amanda Adams, both 12 years old and sixth-grade students at Lakewood Hills Elementary.

Christopher Collins, the popular, blond, blue-eyed sleuth of 128 Crestview Drive, is better known by his nickname, "Hawkeye." His father, Peter Collins, who is an attorney downtown, explains, "We started calling him Hawkeye many years ago because he notices everything, even tiny details. That's what makes him so good at solving mysteries." His mother, Linda Collins, a real estate agent, agrees: "Yes, but he

Sleuths continued on page 4A

Sleuths continued from page 2A

also started to draw at a very early age. His sketches capture everything he sees. He draws clues or the scene of the crime — or anything else that will help solve a mystery."

Amy Adams, a spitfire with red hair and sparkling green eyes, lives right across the street, at 131 Crestview Drive. Known to many as the star of the track team, she is also a star math student. "She's quick of mind, quick of foot and quick of temper," says her teacher, Ted Bronson, chuckling. "And she's never intimidated." Not only do she and Hawkeye share the same birthday, but also the same love of mysteries.

"If something's wrong," says Amy, leaning on her ten-speed, "you just can't look the other way."

"Right," says Hawkeye, pulling his ever-present sketch pad and pencil from his back pocket. "And if we can't solve a case right away, I'll do a drawing of the scene of the crime. When we study my sketch, we can usually figure out what happened."

When the two detectives are not playing video games or soccer (Hawkeye is the captain of the sixth-grade team), they can often be seen biking around town, making sure justice is done. Occa-

sionally aided by Hawkeye's frisky golden retriever, Nosey, and Amy's six-year-old sister, Lucy, they've solved every case they've handled to date.

How did the two get started in the detective business?

It all started last year at Lakewood Hills Elementary's Career Days. There the two met Sergeant Treadwell, one of Lakewood Hills' best-known policemen. Of Hawkeye and Amy, Sergeant Treadwell proudly brags, "They're terrific. Right after we met, one of the teachers had a whole pile of tests stolen. I sure couldn't figure out who had done it, but Hawkeye did one of his sketches and he and Amy had the case solved in five minutes! You can't fool those two."

Sergeant Treadwell adds: "I don't know what Lakewood Hills ever did without Hawkeye and Amy. They've found a dognapped dog, located stolen video games, and cracked many other tough cases. Why, whenever I have a problem I can't solve, I know just where to go — straight to those two super sleuths!"

> **"They've found a dognapped dog, located stolen video games, and cracked many other tough cases."**

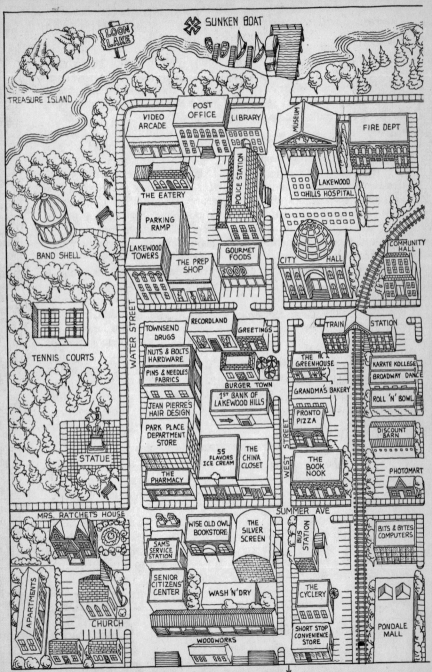

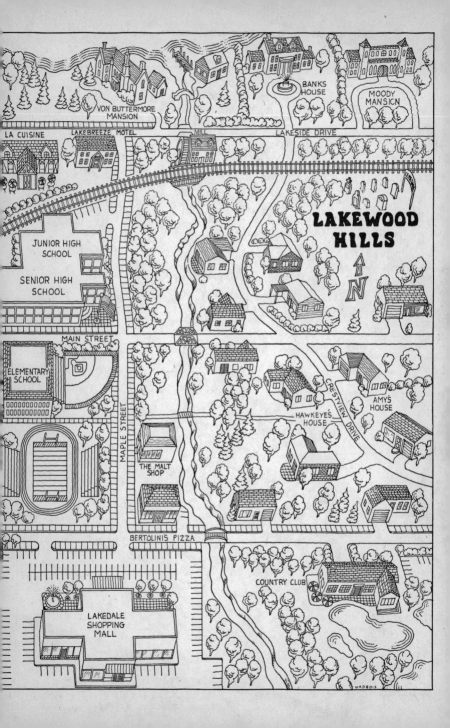

Dear Readers,

You can solve these mysteries along with us! Start by reading very carefully -- Watch out for things like what people say happened, the ways they behave, and details like the time and the weather.

Then look closely at the sketch or other picture clue with the story. If you remember the facts, the picture clue should help you break the case.

If you want to check your answer-- or if a hard case stumps you -- turn to the solutions at the back of the book. They're written in mirror type. Hold them up to a mirror and they'll look right. If you don't have a mirror, turn the page and hold it up to the light. (You can teach yourself to read backwards, too. We can do it prett-- well now and it comes in handy som-- times in our cases.)

Have fun -- we sure did !

Amy

Hawkeye

The Case of the Bragging Boyfriend

"Your mom and dad give the greatest barbecues in town," Hawkeye Collins said to Amy, his best friend. Hawkeye and Amy were well known in Lakewood Hills for solving mysteries. But at the moment, there were no mysteries facing the two 12-year-old sleuths—just food, and lots of it!

They were sitting on the patio in Amy's backyard. The Adams family's annual Labor Day barbecue was in full swing. Family friends, neighbors, and many of Amy's relatives were there. Everybody seemed to be enjoying the good food and lively conversation.

"Yeah, I know." Amy nodded as she munched a plateful of potato chips. "They're really into having cookouts. They even have matching aprons that say 'Born To Barbecue.' Is that corny, or what?"

Hawkeye laughed. "I know. I saw them."

Just then, Amy's little sister, Lucy, flopped down on the wicker chair next to them.

"That guy's a *creep!*" she fumed.

"Who's a creep, Lucy?" Hawkeye asked, wiping crumbs off his alligator T-shirt.

"Laurel's boyfriend, Pete," answered Lucy. "That's the third time he made me get him a plate of burgers and hot dogs. I'm not his slave!"

"Psst . . . Lucy!" warned Amy. "Cool it. They're coming over here."

Amy and Lucy's cousin Laurel was a sophomore at the University of Minnesota. She was short, slim, and pretty, with long brown hair that she kept tossing back over her shoulders. Like most of the guests, Laurel was wearing a T-shirt and shorts. She was clinging to the hand of a very tall, broad-shouldered young man.

"Hi, Amy. Hi, Hawkeye," Laurel said. "This is a great party, isn't it? Have you kids met Pete yet?"

"*I* have," muttered Lucy.

"Hi!" said Pete in a booming voice. He nodded to Amy and held out his hand to Hawkeye. "Real nice to meet you kids," he drawled, pumping Hawkeye's hand vigorously.

"Yeah, it's a thrill and a half meeting you,

too," replied Hawkeye. He withdrew his hand from Pete's powerful grip and gingerly flexed it.

"Hey, sweetheart," Pete said to Lucy, who quickly bent down to look at an imaginary scrape on her knee. "How about getting me another lemonade?" He reached over and gave her a pat on the head. "Whaddya say?"

"Ooh, this scrape really hurts," said Lucy, holding her knee. She closed her eyes tightly and grimaced, as if she were in terrible pain. "I have to get a bandage. Bye." She jumped out of the chair and half-limped, half-hopped quickly into the house. Hawkeye and Amy looked at each other, trying not to burst out laughing.

"Poor little kid," Pete said sympathetically. "Reminds me of the time I fell out of a rowboat on the Colorado River. There I was, all alone, struggling in the rapids. I thought I was done for, but luckily I'm a champion swimmer. I cut myself pretty badly on a sharp rock, but I finally managed to make it to shore.

"Want to see my scar?" he asked, starting to pull up his tight black T-shirt.

"Uh, thanks, but no thanks," Hawkeye answered.

"Pete and I met on a ranch in Wyoming," explained Laurel. "He knows absolutely everything about horses."

Pete tried to look modest. "Yeah. I had a job there this summer catching and taming wild

3

horses. It was fantastic!"

"No kidding?" Amy asked, her green eyes wide. "That's really cool. I love horses. What was it like?"

"Oh, well, it was easy once I got the hang of it," replied Pete. "I mean, I don't like to brag, but there was this one mustang—" Suddenly he snapped his fingers. "But before I tell you about him, I gotta wet my whistle. I'll just get a lemonade and be right back!"

"Isn't he too much?" Laurel asked, watching Pete admiringly as he ambled toward the refreshments. "He's so totally different from all those wimps I was dating last year. I mean, Pete's a real *man!*"

"He's too much all right," agreed Hawkeye sarcastically.

Meanwhile, Lucy limped back to the group, a large bandage covering most of her right knee. She sat down and thrust her knee forward. "Maybe now that guy will leave me alone," she grumbled. Hawkeye and Amy chuckled.

When Pete came back and sat down, he had two large paper cups of lemonade—both for himself.

"Wild horses are OK, but I'm *really* into mountain climbing," he told them between large gulps of lemonade.

"In fact," he continued, "I once had a really hairy time climbing to the top of Mount Everest.

4

I'd been climbing for two hours. I got to ten thousand feet, then twenty thousand feet. My gloves were frozen, I'd lost one of my sneakers, and some of my gear was missing.

"I had to get to the top," Pete went on dramatically, "no matter what. Inch by inch, step by step, I kept climbing. And then, an hour later, I reached the top! I collapsed in the snow, gasping in the thin air at thirty thousand feet!"

"Isn't he too much?" repeated Laurel, looking at Hawkeye and Amy. Amy nodded, her mouth open. Hawkeye just looked thoughtful.

"I even have a picture of myself at the top of the mountain," Pete said, taking a photograph out of his wallet. "I look great, don't I?" he added as the photo was passed around.

When Lucy saw the picture, all she said was "Oh, brother!" Then she stormed off into the house.

"Amy, there's something funny about this photo," Hawkeye whispered. Amy looked at him quizzically.

"Like what?" she asked.

Suddenly, Lucy reappeared. In both hands she held a large watering can. She carefully raised the can and dumped its contents on Pete's head.

"Lucy!" screeched Laurel.

"Why, you little— What'd you do that for?" shouted Pete, rubbing water out of his eyes.

"To get you to cool it with all those dumb

5

"Your boyfriend's a liar and a phony," said Hawkeye quietly.

stories," Lucy retorted angrily.

"I'm telling your mother about this, Lucy," Laurel said after Pete had gone to find a towel. "You had no right to—"

"Hold it, Laurel," said Hawkeye quietly. "I think I know why Lucy's so mad. Your boyfriend's a liar and a phony."

"That's ridiculous," insisted Laurel. "You're just jealous, Hawkeye."

But Hawkeye shook his head and said, "I might be a little jealous—if that mountain-climbing story he told us were true. But it's not!"

HOW DID HAWKEYE KNOW THAT PETE WASN'T TELLING THE TRUTH?

See page 69

The Case of the Splattered Sheets

Hawkeye, Amy, and Amy's little sister, Lucy, were sitting on the grass in Von Buttermore Park. Nosey, Hawkeye's golden retriever, sat in front of her master, wolfing down a doggie treat. It was her reward for retrieving sticks and old tennis balls all afternoon.

"I wish I could get Bernie to do that," said Lucy with a sigh. She picked up a small stick. "C'mon Bernie," she coaxed, waving the stick in front of the big St. Bernard. "Fetch!"

But Bernie just looked at her and blinked his round, soulful eyes. Then he gave a huge yawn and lay down in the grass.

"Forget it, Lucy," Amy said, laughing.

"Bernie's much too lazy!" She scratched the dog behind one ear. "But we love you anyway, Berns."

"I'm not giving up so soon," retorted Lucy, picking up a larger stick. "OK, Bernie—"

But before Lucy could finish her sentence, the St. Bernard clambered to his feet. He looked toward the sidewalk that ran beside the park and started to growl. Nosey was growling, too.

"Hey, I didn't tell you to fetch yet," Lucy protested.

"What is it, Nosey?" Hawkeye asked. "What's the matter, girl?" He got up, brushing grass and twigs from the seat of his jeans.

Suddenly, an enormous black-and-white cat ran down the sidewalk. "Uh-oh," said Hawkeye, "it's Rocky!"

Rocky lived in the grocery store, where he helped to keep the mouse population down. Weighing in at 30 pounds, he spent his days sleeping, fighting, and eating just about anything that came his way. Mr. Johnson, the store owner, tried to keep Rocky inside, but the cat often managed to slip out the door with a departing customer.

Pounding along the sidewalk in pursuit of Rocky came Macho Thornton.

"Why's he chasing Rocky?" asked Amy.

"Who knows," Hawkeye answered, shrugging his shoulders. "He probably just felt like being mean today."

Macho Thornton was in the sixth-grade with

Hawkeye and Amy. He was a bully and a troublemaker. Ever since Hawkeye and Amy had caught him stealing soccer uniforms, he'd gone out of his way to be especially mean to them.

"Stay, girl," commanded Hawkeye, holding on to Nosey's collar. But with a loud bark, Nosey wrenched herself free and took off after Rocky and Macho. Bernie barked, too, but Lucy flung her arms around his neck and clung with all her might, just barely managing to keep him from lumbering off to join the chase.

Amy stood up and shaded her eyes with one hand. "Oh, no! Hawkeye," she cried, "they're heading straight for Mrs. Ratchet's house!"

"And straight for trouble!" Hawkeye groaned. "C'mon, Amy. We'd better try to catch Nosey. You know how Mrs. Ratchet feels about dogs!"

Mrs. Ratchet, who lived alone in a big old house next to the park, was known as the meanest person in Lakewood Hills. She had a definite dislike of trespassers—particularly dogs, cats, and kids.

As Hawkeye and Amy took off at a run, Amy called over her shoulder to Lucy. "You and Bernie stay here in the park till we come back. And keep him out of trouble!"

When Hawkeye and Amy reached Mrs. Ratchet's house, they could hear Nosey barking.

"It's coming from the backyard," Amy said,

and they both ran around to the rear of the house. The first thing they noticed when they got there was that Mrs. Ratchet was nowhere to be seen. The second thing they saw was Macho trying to coax Rocky out of a nearby tree.

Macho turned away from the howling cat. "Oh, it's you turkeys," he said with a nasty smile. "Well, Collins, you're in big trouble this time. Look what your dumb dog did."

Hawkeye, who was trying to quiet the still-barking Nosey, looked over to where Macho was pointing. Amy looked, too. On the ground was half a clothesline of sheets. The other half of the line was still attached to its wooden post.

Just then, Mrs. Ratchet appeared, carrying a bag of groceries. "What are you kids doing in my yard?" she demanded angrily. "Get out, all of you, or I'll call the police."

"Mrs. Ratchet, we—" Hawkeye cautiously began.

But Mrs. Ratchet suddenly saw the line of laundry on the ground. "My sheets!" she screeched, dropping the bag of groceries and rushing over to the clothesline. Then she glared at Hawkeye, Amy, and Macho. "All right, which one of you juvenile delinquents is responsible for this?"

"I saw the whole thing, ma'am," Macho said in a sugary voice. "It was Hawkeye's pooch, Dozey. She was chasing that poor cat, and she ran into the clothesline and knocked it down with her paws. It was all her fault!"

"Mrs. Ratchet, that's impossible," Hawkeye said firmly. "Nosey is too well trained. She'd never—"

"This is the last straw!" interrupted Mrs. Ratchet. "My arthritis is bothering me and my daughter is coming to visit—and now I have to wash my sheets all over again! Your parents will be hearing from me, Hawkeye Collins. And the dog pound, too!" And with a final angry look at Hawkeye and Nosey, Mrs. Ratchet picked up her groceries and stormed into her house.

"Gee, that's too bad, Collins," said Macho, shaking his head. "Sorry I can't stick around. See you turkeys later.

"Hey, Collins!" he added as he elbowed his way through the tall bushes around Mrs. Ratchet's house. "Maybe you should get a hamster or something."

"I'm getting *you* a snake," yelled Amy, her fists clenched. "To match your personality!"

"Forget about him," Hawkeye told her. "Somehow we have to convince Mrs. Ratchet that Nosey's innocent."

"Really," Amy agreed, concern replacing the anger in her eyes. "But how?"

Together they surveyed the sorry scene. The sheets on the ground were mud-stained.

"It looks bad for Nosey," said Amy, her hands on her hips.

13

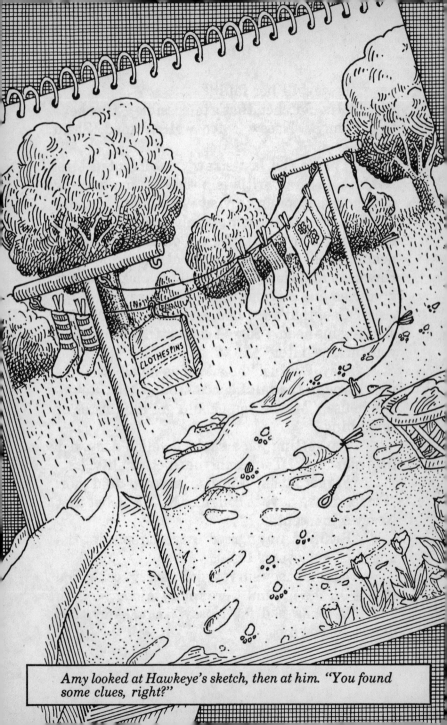

Amy looked at Hawkeye's sketch, then at him. "You found some clues, right?"

"You wouldn't do a thing like that, would you, girl?" Hawkeye said, bending down to pet Nosey. Nosey looked at her master with adoring eyes. She was quiet now that Rocky had somehow managed to climb down from the tree and had waddled off toward home.

Hawkeye took his sketch pad out of his back pocket and rapidly began to draw the downed clothesline and sheets. When he finished the sketch, he studied it thoughtfully, then suddenly snapped his fingers.

Amy looked at him and grinned. "Hawkeye, you found some clues, right?"

"Absolutely! This sure ought to convince Mrs. Ratchet that Nosey couldn't possibly have wrecked her sheets!"

WHAT WAS IN HAWKEYE'S SKETCH THAT PROVED NOSEY WAS INNOCENT?

S O L U T I O N
See page 71

The Mystery of the Telltale Timepiece

It was a crisp, cool Saturday morning in early fall. Hawkeye and Amy, dressed in down vests and light wool sweaters, were on their way to the shopping mall. They planned to spend the morning browsing through the new discount record store that had just opened.

As they rode their bikes into the mall parking lot, they spotted Sergeant Treadwell. Sarge was their special friend, and they often helped him with his cases. He was standing in front of Traynor's Electronics, one of the few stores in the mall that had an outside entrance. The Sergeant had both hands on his hips and was looking at something on the ground. He was shaking his head slowly from side to side.

"Sarge doesn't look very happy," said Hawkeye. "I wonder what's up."

"Let's check it out," Amy replied.

As Amy and Hawkeye approached the store, they saw what Sergeant Treadwell had been staring at. Broken glass littered the ground. When they looked around for the source of the glass, they saw a large, jagged hole in the electronics store window.

"Oh, man! What a mess!" exclaimed Amy. "Sarge, what happened?"

"It looks like a smash and grab robbery," Sarge explained. "Sometime after midnight, a thief threw a rock through the window, grabbed some cameras and calculators from the display, and ran."

"Didn't the burglar alarm go off?" Amy wanted to know.

Sarge shook his head. "It was broken. Mr. Traynor was planning to have it fixed today."

"How do you know the robbery happened after midnight, Sarge?" asked Hawkeye, carefully picking bits of glass from the bottom of his running shoe.

"The ice cream shop next door closes at midnight on Fridays," said Sarge. "The manager passed by on the way to his car. According to him, the area was deserted."

"Could *he* have done it?" asked Amy.

"No, his story checks out. An officer on night patrol saw him drive away."

"Any suspects, Sarge?" Hawkeye asked.

Before Sergeant Treadwell could answer, Mr. Traynor, the store's owner, came toward them, nervously clutching a piece of paper.

"Here's a complete list of the stolen items, Sergeant," he said. "I do hope you'll be able to apprehend the hoodlum." He mopped his forehead with a large white handkerchief. "It's simply awful. Some of my most expensive cameras. . . ."

"Mr. Traynor here claims he saw two people staring in the window for a really long time yesterday afternoon," said Sarge. "One was Josh Evans, and the other—"

"Josh!" Amy broke in. "You've got to be kidding! Josh is no thief!" Her green eyes flashed angrily.

Josh Evans, the manager of the Video Arcade, was well liked by all the kids in town, and Amy and Hawkeye thought of him as a special friend. It was hard for Amy to believe that he could be involved in a crime.

"Cool it, Amy," cautioned Hawkeye. "Let Sarge finish, OK?"

"As I was saying," Sarge continued, "the other suspect is Mike Graham, a former employee of Mr. Traynor's, who now works as a stock clerk at Soames Clothing Store."

"He was a pretty good worker, I'll say that

much for him," put in Mr. Traynor. "I wasn't at all happy when he quit."

"I talked to both Josh and Mike concerning their whereabouts after midnight," continued Sarge. "Josh claims he was asleep until about three-thirty. Then he got up to go fishing with his friend Charlie Laub at Loon Lake. He says they were out on the lake fishing from four o'clock to five-thirty, and they have the fish to prove it.

"He also says he was looking in the window here yesterday afternoon trying to decide whether or not to buy his girl friend the digital wristwatch Mr. Traynor had on display."

"And the *other* guy?" Amy asked impatiently.

"Mike claims he was sleeping until five o'clock this morning. Then he went to the Eatery, which has begun serving an early breakfast, before starting work at Soames. He was at the Eatery from five-thirty to six-thirty and can prove it. He also claims he was nowhere near here yesterday afternoon."

"One of them might be lying," said Hawkeye thoughtfully.

"That's right," agreed Sarge. "But *who's* lying, and when did the crime take place?" He looked at Hawkeye and Amy and shrugged his shoulders. "I'm stumped.

"Well, I've got to get back to the station," said Sarge. He glanced down at his wrist. "Oh, heck, my watch's stopped. Does anyone know what time it is?"

"It's eleven o'clock," Mr. Traynor replied, looking at the wall clock inside his store. "And you can be sure that's the exact time. All my watches and clocks are accurate to the minute."

Hawkeye and Amy walked with Sarge to his squad car. As Sarge got in, he said to the sleuths, "If you two find out anything, let me know. I'm really stumped on this one." And, shaking his head regretfully, he drove off.

"Come on, Amy," said Hawkeye. "Let's go back and check out that broken window. There might be some clue Sarge overlooked."

"Yeah," Amy replied, "and I sure hope we find something that will clear Josh!"

Hawkeye and Amy peered carefully into the gaping hole. A small computer monitor and keyboard stood on the topmost shelf of the display. A few other items lay scattered around the bottom shelf.

Hawkeye whipped out his sketch pad and pencil and quickly drew a sketch of the window display. As he was putting in the last few lines, his eyes lit up. He showed the drawing to Amy, who looked at it closely.

"Well?" asked Hawkeye, grinning. "Do you see what I see?"

"For sure!" Amy answered. "And it definitely proves which suspect is telling the truth, and

"Let's show Sarge how we've 'unstumped' the case for him," said Hawkeye.

which one might be lying."

"Let's go to the police station and show Sarge the sketch," Hawkeye said. "He'll be really happy when he finds out we've 'unstumped' the case for him!"

HOW DID HAWKEYE AND AMY KNOW WHICH SUSPECT WAS INNOCENT?

See page 73

The Case of the Computer Cutup

School had just finished for the day. Hawkeye and Amy were standing outside the building talking to Corey Callahan, who had just moved to Lakewood Hills. Corey was small and thin with red hair that was a shade darker than Amy's. Hawkeye and Amy had noticed that Corey never seemed to be able to stay still for very long. Even while they talked, he restlessly zipped and unzipped his bright blue nylon jacket.

At the moment, they were trading likes and dislikes.

"Hey, I'm into soccer, too," Corey told them. "And you can give me a pepperoni pizza anytime," he said, agreeing with Hawkeye's choice of a favorite food. "Puzzles and mysteries are great, and I really love a good joke," he added, grinning.

Amy grinned back. "I like all those things, too. But you can definitely leave the pepperoni off *my* pizza!"

"I like working with computers best, though," Corey went on, "especially making up my own computer games and puzzles."

"You should talk to Hawkeye," Amy replied, pointing to her friend. "He makes up computer games, too, and he's really good at it!"

"Oh, come on, Amy," said Hawkeye. "Cool it, will you?"

"Hey, that's great!" Corey exclaimed excitedly. "You two should come over to my house sometime soon. We can play my latest game, Crazymaze. But I'm warning you guys—I always win!"

"Want to bet you won't this time?" challenged Amy with a mischievous smile.

"OK, you're on," said Corey. "How about tomorrow afternoon after school, at my house? I'll provide the pizza—no pepperoni, I promise. Is tomorrow OK?"

Amy nodded. "Fine with me. Hawkeye?"

"I'm game," Hawkeye said, his eyes twinkling.

Amy rolled her eyes and groaned at his bad joke.

"Hey, I have to get going," Corey said, laughing. He picked up his backpack and carelessly slung it over his shoulder. "See you guys tomorrow, right?" And with a final grin, Corey bounded down the steps and ran toward the bike racks.

"Let's go over to the Video Arcade and get in a couple of games," Hawkeye suggested. "We need practice!"

"Good idea," agreed Amy, who was rummaging through her backpack. "Oh, rats!" she exclaimed. "I left my new aviator sunglasses in the computer room. Meet you at the arcade in fifteen minutes."

Amy reentered the building and dashed down the hall toward the computer room. When she got to the door, she saw Sally Chan and Mike Garcia inside. Like Hawkeye and Amy, they were members of the Bytes of Data Computer Club.

Mike and Sally were standing next to one of the computers. Mike had his hands on his hips and was glaring at Sally. Sally's face was pale with anger.

"I didn't touch your stupid disk or your computer," Sally was saying. "I just got here. I don't even know what you're talking about!"

"Hey, what's going on?" Amy asked as she came into the room.

"Sally messed up the program I wrote yesterday. That's what's going on," fumed Mike. Sally opened her mouth to defend herself again, but Amy stopped her.

"Hold on a minute, Sally," she said. "Exactly what happened, when did it happen, and how come you're blaming Sally?" Amy asked Mike.

"About half an hour ago, I came in here to look at the program I wrote yesterday during the meeting," explained Mike. "You know, the shot-on-goal percentages for the soccer team this year. The coach asked me to do it, remember?" Amy nodded.

"Well," Mike continued, "everything was working fine—at first. I typed up my program to load and then hit the return key. But instead of soccer percentages, I got this!" He pointed to the computer screen.

For the first time, Amy and Sally looked at the computer. Part of the screen showed the name of the computer program—Visi-Comp—and the name of Mike's program—Coach. That part looked normal. But underneath was the strangest message Amy had ever seen.

"This is definitely weird," said Amy, shaking her head slowly.

"It sure is," Sally agreed.

"And Sally is the only one who could have done it," insisted Mike. "She stayed late yesterday, after everyone had left, to finish her program. Well, she sure finished me!"

"Oh, come on, Mike. Anyone could have reprogrammed that disk between yesterday afternoon and the time you got here today," Amy

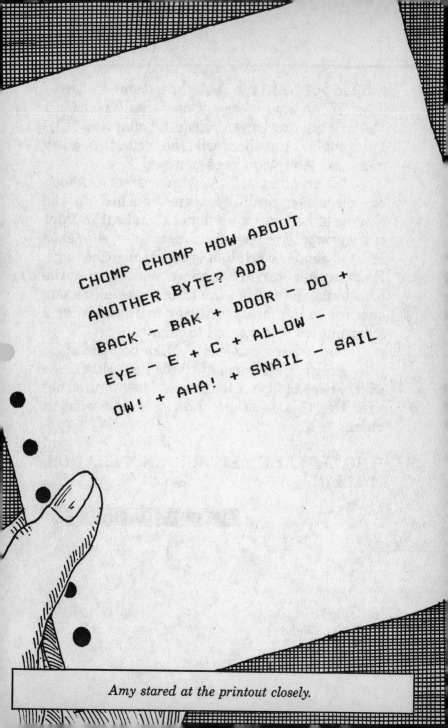

CHOMP CHOMP HOW ABOUT
ANOTHER BYTE? ADD
BACK - BAK + DOOR - DO +
EYE - E + C + ALLOW -
OW! + AHA! + SNAIL - SAIL

Amy stared at the printout closely.

pointed out. "Anyone could have come in here."

"Yeah, and it wasn't me," Sally insisted.

"Well, maybe you're right," admitted Mike grudgingly. "But then, who did write that crazy message? And what does it mean?"

"Good question," Amy answered. She took off her green corduroy blazer, pushed up the sleeves of her cotton turtleneck, and sat in front of the computer screen. A moment later, she asked Mike to get her a printout of the strange message. Propping her chin in her hands, she stared at the printout closely. Then she traced carefully along one line of the message with her finger. After a few minutes, she started to laugh.

"So, what's the joke?" Mike demanded.

Amy turned around to face him. "Mike," she said between gulps of laughter, "I just figured out who left this message. I even know what it means!"

WHO LEFT THE MESSAGE, AND WHAT DID IT MEAN?

See page 77

The Secret of the Loon Lake Monster

"Monster! Monster!" a woman screamed, running toward Hawkeye and Amy, who were collecting rocks along the shore of Loon Lake.

The young detectives looked up and saw a large woman with tightly curled blue-gray hair closing in on them. Her bright yellow shorts and orange-flowered blouse almost made their eyes hurt.

"Oh, no!" Hawkeye groaned. "Grab a net! Here comes another 'Loonie Bird'!"

Amy chuckled and muttered out of the side of her mouth, "Watch it, Hawk. She's headed right for us!"

The Loon Lake Resort was crowded with

sightseers eager for a look at "Loonie," the lake monster that had been seen and photographed by the resort owner, Mr. Babbit.

The woman waved her arm wildly toward the middle of the lake and yelled, "Look! There it is!"

Amy and Hawkeye shaded their eyes and peered into the glare of the late afternoon sun on the water.

"Wow!" breathed Hawkeye, pointing to the middle of the lake. "Amy, look! I see something!" he said excitedly.

"You're kidding!" Amy ran closer to the water's edge for a better look.

After a minute of tense concentration on a dark shape in the lake, she declared, "Hawkeye, it's just a log! It isn't even moving. And it has branches and leaves on the end."

"I'm sure I saw it move," the woman said. "Are you looking in the right place?" She frowned into the bright light.

After a moment, the woman sighed. "I guess you're right," she said disappointedly. "I thought for sure I'd seen Loonie. I wanted to be the next person to spot the monster."

Hawkeye picked up a smooth stone. "Lots of people *think* they've seen it, but I wonder how many Loonies are really logs," he said. He sent the stone skipping across the water. "So far, Mr. Babbit's the only one who's seen it up close."

"Wasn't it lucky he had his camera ready when the monster came to the surface?" the woman asked, still looking over the water. "Imagine seeing it *and* getting a picture to prove it!"

"Lucky's too mild a word," said Amy under her breath. "Miraculous is more like it."

"Well," the woman said, "I've got to go. My husband and I are taking a boat ride to see if we can get a look at Loonie before dinner." Amy and Hawkeye watched the woman hurry down the wooden dock and board a crowded sight-seeing boat.

"I wonder if there really *is* a monster in Loon Lake," Amy murmured. "What do you think?" She stooped to pick up a piece of granite and rubbed her thumb over the rough rock.

Hawkeye shrugged. "I don't know. Lake Champlain has Champ, and Loch Ness has Nessie," he said, taking off his glasses and polishing them on his Minnesota Vikings T-shirt. "I guess Loon Lake could have something, too. But I'd be more convinced if I saw it myself."

He put his glasses back on. "It's all so sudden. You'd think if there were anything in the lake, we'd have heard about it before now."

"Monster or not, business here at the resort has sure picked up," Amy observed. "Remember last year? There were maybe a dozen families here at the lake. Now the place is packed."

"True." A man's voice behind them made

Hawkeye and Amy spin around. "Loonie certainly has brought the people out, all right." The pudgy, balding man smiled at the pair. "I'm Clarence Babbit. I own this resort—and I took the famous photograph of Loonie.

"I don't like to intrude," he continued, "but I couldn't help overhearing you two. Sounds like you don't believe in Loonie. We can't have that, now, can we?" Mr. Babbit reached out to tousle Hawkeye's hair, but Hawkeye ducked away.

"Let me show you my picture," the resort owner said eagerly. "Have you heard how I took it?"

Before Hawkeye or Amy could answer, Mr. Babbit pulled a photograph out of his pocket and held it up for their inspection.

"It was about four-thirty in the afternoon when I snapped this," he explained, handing the print to Amy. "I was standing about halfway out on the pier over there." He pointed toward the wooden dock. "I heard some splashing, and when I looked up, I saw the creature! I was so surprised, I almost forgot I had my camera with me."

Amy handed the photo to Hawkeye and looked out across the water.

"I got a real good shot, though," Mr. Babbit said, gesturing toward the picture in Hawkeye's hand.

Amy scratched her head and said, "Your resort's gotten a lot of publicity out of this, hasn't it?"

"Let me show you my picture," the resort owner said
eagerly.

Mr. Babbit got out a handkerchief and mopped his brow. "I guess you could say that," he admitted. "The picture's been in quite a few papers. And lots of people have come forward now to say that they've seen Loonie, too."

"Mr. Babbit," Amy said, shaking her head, "I don't know what anyone else has seen, but I do know that you didn't photograph any lake monster off the pier. That picture's a phony!"

HOW DID AMY KNOW MR. BABBIT WASN'T TELLING THE TRUTH?

See page 81

The Case of the Nabbed Necklace

Hawkeye and Amy wandered through the halls of the Lakewood Hills Art Museum. Even though it was only the middle of the afternoon, all the museum's lights were on. A fierce thunderstorm was raging outside, and as Amy and Hawkeye passed a window, they could see rain beating against the glass.

"I sure hope the storm stops by the time we leave," Amy muttered.

"For sure," Hawkeye replied, "or else it'll be a real bummer riding home!"

"Let's go look at the horse drawings," Amy said. "They're my favorite part of the museum."

As they turned a corner, they noticed a few

people standing around a table. On the table was an oval display case.

"I bet that's the diamond necklace the museum just got," Hawkeye said.

"How did you know the museum was getting a necklace?" asked Amy curiously.

"I heard about it on TV last night," Hawkeye answered. "Some museum in New York loaned it to Lakewood Hills for a couple of months. The necklace even has its own special guard, who travels with it."

"Let's check it out," suggested Amy.

They walked over to the display and looked at the necklace. It was mounted on a velvet-covered pedestal.

Hawkeye read from a card that was taped to the glass: " 'Diamond and emerald necklace, circa 1769. Once worn by the Empress Maria Theresa of Austria.' "

"Wow!" he exclaimed. "I've never seen so many diamonds before!"

"Neither have I," Amy agreed. "Boy, they sure knew how to get dressed up in those days!" she added, looking down at her faded blue corduroys and scuffed moccasins.

"They probably weren't too comfortable wearing all that jewelry," Hawkeye reminded her. "And I read somewhere that dresses back then weighed a ton!"

Hawkeye and Amy stared at the glittering

necklace for a few more minutes. They were about to move on when a booming crack of thunder suddenly shook the room, and the lights went out. Then they heard someone scream and the sound of footsteps fading into the distance.

When the lights flickered back on, Hawkeye and Amy saw a woman on the floor. They rushed over to her.

"What happened, ma'am?" Hawkeye asked as he helped her up.

"I . . . I'm not sure," replied the woman as she picked up her purse. "When the lights went out, someone crashed into me and knocked me down!"

"Hawkeye!" cried Amy. "The necklace! It's gone!"

Just then, Mr. Bagley, the curator of the museum, came running into the room. "I heard a scream," he said. "What happened?"

Without waiting for an answer, he looked over at the display case. "Oh, no!" he exclaimed. "Someone's stolen the necklace!

"I knew I should have had an extra alarm installed," he moaned, clutching the table with both hands. "I told them our regular security system plus even the special guard wouldn't be enough." Then he looked up at the ceiling. "Oh, how am I ever going to explain this to the museum in New York?"

Frantically, he glanced around the room.

"Did you see who did it?" he asked Hawkeye and Amy.

"It happened when the lights went out," Hawkeye told him. "We didn't see *anything!*"

"We did hear some footsteps," Amy put in. "But it was hard to tell which way they were going."

Suddenly, Hawkeye jerked up his head and looked around the room. "What's that?" he asked abruptly.

"It sounds like someone groaning," replied Amy.

"It's coming from that room," cried Hawkeye, pointing to a door that was marked PRIVATE. "C'mon, Amy! Mr. Bagley! Quick!"

When the three of them burst into the small room, they saw a man dressed in a guard's uniform sitting in a chair. He was holding his head in his hands and groaning.

"Joe!" Mr. Bagley said. "What happened?"

There was no response from the guard.

"Joe!" repeated Mr. Bagley.

This time, the guard raised his head, looking somewhat startled. Then he grimaced with pain. "I was sitting at my desk when the lights went out," he explained. "Then somebody conked me on the head! One moment I was erasing a wrong answer in a crossword puzzle, and the next thing I knew, my head was down on the desk, and I was coming to.

"There's something weird about all this," said Amy.

"When I looked up," the guard continued, "I saw a flash of lightning. It lit up the room for a second. I could barely make out a shadowy figure climbing out the window over there." He pointed to an open window on the opposite side of the room.

"I've got to report the robbery to the police right away!" said Mr. Bagley. "And Joe, you'd better get some ice for your head."

After Joe and Mr. Bagley left, Hawkeye and Amy looked around the room for clues.

"There's something weird about all this," said Amy, chewing thoughtfully on a fingernail.

"Yeah," Hawkeye agreed. "I wonder if—"

He stopped in midsentence and stood completely still, thinking hard. Then, shaking his head, he whipped out his sketch pad and quickly drew a sketch of the room.

He studied the sketch a moment, then snapped his fingers.

"There's *definitely* something weird about all this!" he said to Amy. "See what I mean?"

"Sure do," Amy replied, grinning. Her green eyes sparkled. "I think we've caught our thief!"

WHO DO THEY SUSPECT STOLE THE NECKLACE?

See page 83

The Secret of the Concealed Cash

"Here it is, Mrs. von Buttermore," Hawkeye said. "It was buried in the garden, next to a rosebush." He held up the diamond collar belonging to Priceless, Mrs. von Buttermore's Great Dane. The collar was wet and muddy, and the gold clasp was broken.

Hawkeye and Amy were standing in the drawing room of the von Buttermore mansion. Mrs. von Buttermore, the richest woman in Lakewood Hills, was sitting on an antique velvet sofa.

"Poor Priceless," sighed Mrs. von Buttermore. "I knew the collar was bothering him, but I didn't realize he'd go so far as to bury it!

"Hawkeye and Amy, I can't thank you

enough," she continued. "I do hope you'll stay for lunch. You must be starving!"

The two sleuths looked at each other and smiled happily.

"Thanks a lot, Mrs. von Buttermore," Amy replied. "That'd be great!"

Mrs. von Buttermore pressed a small button on the wall, and almost immediately, a maid came into the room.

"You rang, madam?" she asked.

"Yes, Maggie," replied Mrs. von Buttermore. "There will be two guests for lunch today. Please set up the oak table next to the fireplace."

"Certainly, madam," Maggie replied.

Just then, a respectful tap was heard at the door. Mrs. von Buttermore called, "Come in," and a tall, dignified-looking man in a tuxedo entered the room. It was Henry, the butler.

"I went to the bank, as you instructed, madam, and withdrew two fifty-dollar bills for your nephew, Master Nick," he said. "The money is in an envelope on the hall table, next to the birthday card. The card awaits your signature."

"Oh, thank you, Henry," said Mrs. von Buttermore. Bowing slightly, the butler left the room, followed closely by the maid.

"Oh, wow!" exclaimed Hawkeye. "I just thought of something! Amy, my parents said something about taking us out to lunch, remember? I'd better call them."

"Are you sure it's all right for you to stay, Hawkeye?" asked Mrs. von Buttermore anxiously.

"No sweat," answered Hawkeye. "Mom and Dad are really nice about things like this."

"The phone is right at the top of the stairs," said Mrs. von Buttermore. "Do you want Henry or Maggie to show you the way?"

"No, I think I can find it OK," Hawkeye said as he walked toward the door. "Don't start lunch without me!"

"We'll try not to," Amy teasingly called after him.

"Right, Mom. I'll be sure and thank Mrs. von Buttermore. See you later. Bye." Hawkeye hung up the phone and started back down the staircase, counting steps as he went. When he got to the tenth step, he suddenly stopped short, not daring to breathe.

In the hall below him was Maggie, the maid. Hawkeye saw her take an envelope from the hall table and put it into her apron pocket. Then she picked up a large dustcloth and scurried into the library.

Hawkeye let out a huge breath. "I can't believe it!" he gasped. "I'd better go tell Mrs. von Buttermore!"

Amy and Mrs. von Buttermore were looking at photos when Hawkeye burst breathlessly into the room.

"What's wrong?" Mrs. von Buttermore asked.

"You look like you just saw a ghost," said Amy. "What happened?"

Hawkeye hesitated for a moment before answering. Would Mrs. von Buttermore believe him? He had to take the chance.

"You know the envelope of money Mr. Hobbs left on the hall table?" he asked her. She nodded. "Well, I just saw your maid, Maggie, steal it!"

"Hawkeye, that's impossible," said Mrs. von Buttermore with a laugh. "Maggie wouldn't do that. You must have been seeing things."

Hawkeye shook his head slowly. "No, Mrs. von Buttermore. I'm sorry, but she really did take the money."

"But the agency recommended her to me very highly," Mrs. von Buttermore said. "And she had excellent references. Hawkeye, couldn't you be mistaken?"

"I'm not, Mrs. von Buttermore," Hawkeye insisted stubbornly. "I know what I saw!"

There was a pause. Then Amy, who had been looking closely at Hawkeye, said, "Maybe Maggie just took the money by accident. Why don't we go ask her? Hawkeye, where did you say she went?"

"I didn't, but she went into the library," answered Hawkeye abruptly.

On their way into the library, they passed

the hall table. Hawkeye silently pointed to the birthday card and the empty space where the money had been.

Maggie was busily dusting a tall row of bookshelves when Hawkeye, Amy, and Mrs. von Buttermore entered the library.

"Oh, Maggie, here you are," said Mrs. von Buttermore. "I'd like to ask you something."

"Certainly, madam," replied the maid. "What is it?"

"Some money is missing from the table in the hall. Is it possible you might have picked it up by mistake?"

Maggie turned bright red. "Are you accusing me of stealing?" she asked angrily.

"No, Maggie," said Mrs. von Buttermore quietly. "I just wondered if—"

"I didn't take any money," insisted the maid. She thrust her hand into her apron pocket and turned the pocket inside out. "See? I don't have it!"

"Well, Hawkeye?" asked Mrs. von Buttermore. "You can see that Maggie doesn't have it."

"But I saw her take it!" Hawkeye insisted. "I'm positive she's lying!"

"Lying?" screeched the maid. She glared first at Hawkeye, then at Mrs. von Buttermore. "I've never been so insulted in my life! I quit!" She threw the dustcloth on the floor and stomped out of the room, banging the door behind her.

"Boy, she sure was mad," murmured Amy

Robinson Crusoe - Daniel Defoe
Selected Poems - Emily Dickinson
A Christmas Carol - Charles Dickens
David Copperfield - Charles Dickens
Nicholas Nickleby - Charles Dickens
Oliver Twist - Charles Dickens
A Tale Of Two Cities - Charles Dickens
The Adventures Of Sherlock Holmes - A. Conan Doyle

Hawkeye made a list of the books on the dusted shelf.

as she twisted a strand of her red hair around her finger. "Are you sure you saw her, Hawkeye?"

Hawkeye had to convince Mrs. von Buttermore he was telling the truth—but how?

He looked around the room for a moment. Then he walked over to the bookshelves the maid had been dusting. He pulled out a couple of books, flipped through them carefully, then put them back on the shelf.

"Hawkeye, you can't look through every book in here," said Amy. "There are too many."

"You're right," Hawkeye answered. "Mrs. von Buttermore, if I find the missing money, will you believe me?"

"Of course, Hawkeye," Mrs. von Buttermore answered uncertainly.

Hawkeye nodded, then pulled out his sketch pad and started making a list of the books on the dusted shelf. After a few moments, he turned around, a big grin on his face.

"Mrs. von Buttermore, you can close the book on this case," he said. "I know exactly where the maid hid the money."

WHERE DID THE MAID HIDE THE MONEY?

See page 87

The Mystery of the Midnight Trickster

"Hawkeye, it's happened again!"

Hawkeye looked up from his hand-held video game to see his friend and tentmate, Paul Shimamoto, enter their tent and flop down on his sleeping bag. "This camping trip is turning out to be a nightmare!" Paul exclaimed.

Hawkeye, Paul, and some of their fellow campers from Computer Camp had canoed across the lake to a special campsite for a two-day sleepover. Everyone had expected to have a good time swimming, fishing, or just plain relaxing, but now it looked like someone was determined to ruin the fun by pulling tricks on the campers.

"Who got it this time?" Hawkeye asked.

"Jerry Kaplan," said Paul. "Just now, when he went to put on his sneakers, they were full of rocks."

Hawkeye shook his head. "First Chuck McCarthy finds a frog in his backpack. Then Keith gets up yesterday morning and finds all his socks tied together."

"Boy, was he mad!" exclaimed Paul, remembering the angry expression on their counselor's face.

"He got even madder last night when he found out somebody'd replaced the marshmallows with cotton balls," Hawkeye reminded him.

Paul scratched a mosquito bite on his leg. "I like a good joke as well as the next guy, but these tricks are really dumb."

"Yeah," agreed Hawkeye as he gingerly picked up his sneakers, checking them carefully to see if anything strange had been put inside. "I may have a way to find out who's been pulling these stunts," he announced.

"You have? How?" Paul asked.

"I'll tell you after dinner," Hawkeye promised.

After dinner, everybody sat around the campfire toasting marshmallows, real ones this time. The sun was just starting to go down, and an eerie orange and pink glow filtered through the surrounding trees.

"This fire's too hot!" Chris Rabosky complained, for what seemed like the tenth time. He was sitting slightly away from the group, putting calamine lotion all over his arms and legs. "And this dumb poison ivy still itches like crazy!"

"No one told you to stash the canoe paddles in a patch of poison ivy, Chris," replied Keith quietly.

"How was I supposed to know what that stuff was?" Chris retorted, then went on muttering angrily to himself. "This place stinks. No real beds, crummy food, and worst of all, no computers!"

When the group broke up a little later and the campers went to their tents, Paul and Hawkeye held a quiet conversation.

"Everybody thinks it's Chris Rabosky who's playing all these tricks," Paul said. "Even Keith thinks so."

"It could be Chris," Hawkeye said thoughtfully. "I mean, all he's done since we got here is complain.

"Anyway," he continued, "whoever's doing it must be sneaking out of his tent at night when we're all asleep, right?"

Paul nodded. "Right. So?"

"So my plan is to stay up all night, watch the campsite, and try to catch our mystery trickster in the act." Hawkeye looked out of the tent. "There's supposed to be a full moon tonight, too, so it should be pretty easy to see anyone who's sneaking around the camp."

"Well, wake me up if you catch him," Paul said, yawning. He lay down on top of his sleeping bag and was soon fast asleep.

Hawkeye lay down on his sleeping bag, too, on his stomach, his head facing the opening of the tent. From that position, he had a good view of much of the campsite. Hawkeye noticed that because of the hot night, a lot of kids had dragged their sleeping bags halfway outside their tents. Like Paul, they were lying on top of their sleeping bags. Everyone seemed to be asleep.

To pass the time, Hawkeye decided to make a sketch of the campsite. He reached for his backpack as quietly as he could and took out his sketch pad. The moon hadn't risen yet, but there was still enough light from the campfire so that he could see what he was doing.

Hawkeye worked quickly but carefully. He drew Tommy Spano's tent, which was close to his own, and sketched Tommy's feet, which were sticking out of the front of his tent. Then he drew what was visible of Jerry Kaplan's head in his tent opening.

After Hawkeye finished his drawing, he put down his sketch pad and pencil and yawned. "I *have* to stay awake," he muttered drowsily. But it was no use. After a few seconds, his head drooped down onto the sleeping bag, and he fell asleep.

A while later, Hawkeye woke up with a start.

Someone outside was yelling.

"Hey, what's going on?" Paul asked in a groggy voice.

"Beats me," answered Hawkeye, rubbing his eyes. He crawled out of the tent and stood up. It was still dark, but a full moon was shining brightly. Over by Keith's tent, Hawkeye could see Keith and Chris Rabosky.

"I thought it was you, Rabosky!" the counselor shouted angrily. "What were you planning to do this time—pull the tent stakes out of the ground?"

"I wasn't going to do anything!" Chris shouted back. "I was just on my way down to the lake to fill my canteen." He held the canteen up in front of Keith's face, turned it upside down, and shook it. "See?" he said. "It's empty."

By this time, everyone had gotten up and was crowding around Keith and Chris.

"Why don't you just admit it, Chris?" said Tommy Spano, who was standing next to Hawkeye. "You got caught red-handed!"

"All right, all right, you guys," Keith said wearily. "Let's go back to bed. We'll talk about this in the morning, OK?"

Reluctantly, the campers walked back to their tents. Suddenly, Tommy Spano started to howl. "Yow!" he yelled, hopping up and down on one bare foot. "That's the second time tonight I've stubbed my toe on one of these stupid tent stakes!"

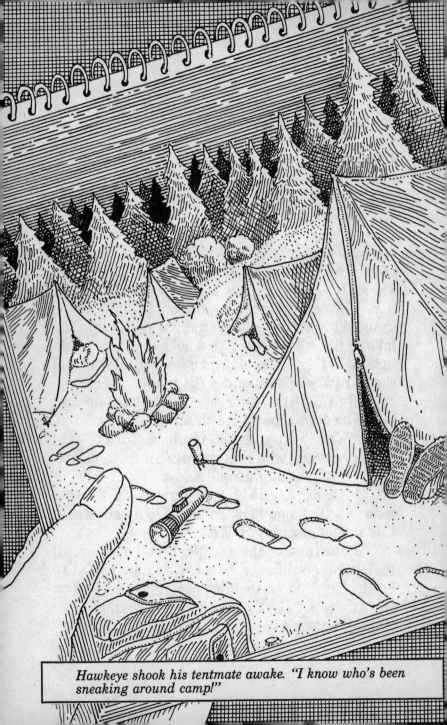

Hawkeye shook his tentmate awake. "I know who's been sneaking around camp!"

When Hawkeye got back to his tent, he lay down on his sleeping bag and stared into the darkness. Paul was already asleep, but Hawkeye couldn't stop thinking about what had just happened. "Something doesn't add up," he muttered. "But what is it?"

He sat up and got his flashlight out of his backpack. He picked up the sketch he had drawn earlier that evening. "Wait a minute," he said. He looked out of the tent and across the campsite. Then he looked at the sketch again.

"Paul!" he whispered, shaking his friend gently. "Wake up!"

"Huh? What's the big idea?" Paul mumbled.

"I can't prove who's been playing all those pranks," Hawkeye told him, "but I know who's been sneaking around camp tonight—and I'll bet he and the trickster are one and the same!"

HOW DID HAWKEYE KNOW WHO THE MIDNIGHT TRICKSTER MIGHT BE?

See page 89

The Case of the Camera Snatcher

A few days after Hawkeye got back from camp, he and Amy spent part of the afternoon sitting through a new science fiction movie called *Bylar: the Beast from Planet X.*

"Boy, that's the last time I listen to a rave review from Marsha," said Amy after the movie had ended and they were coming out of the theater into the hot sun. "That was the worst movie I've ever seen!"

"It sure was," Hawkeye agreed. "The only good thing about it was the air conditioning in the theater!"

"I'll say," Amy replied. She reached down into the pocket of her khaki shorts. "Hey, I've got some money left! Let's go across the street and get some ice cream."

As they headed toward the 55 Flavors Ice Cream shop, an old bum who was coming the other way bumped into Amy.

"Oops, excuse me, mister," she said politely. Then she did a double take at the bum and exclaimed, "Sarge! It's you! How come you're in disguise again?"

"Yeah, what's going on, Sarge?" Hawkeye asked.

Sarge was wearing a ragged shirt, a pair of worn wool pants, and a stained wool jacket that he had just barely managed to button across his large stomach. A bushy white wig and pasted-on white eyebrows completed his disguise.

"Ssh!" he whispered, looking down at the sidewalk and adjusting his eyebrows. "Sorry I didn't see you, Amy. Act like you don't know who I am."

"No way, Sarge. We know who you are now," Amy said impatiently, "so you might as well tell us what's up."

"OK, OK," said Sarge. He looked around, then pointed to the alleyway next to the movie theater. "Let's talk over there," he said. "It's safer."

When they got to the alleyway, Sarge said, "Maybe you can help me out. I'm stalking a 'snatcher.'"

"A what?" Amy asked.

"A snatcher is a thief who steals purses, chain jewelry, cameras—things that can be grabbed from someone's shoulder or neck," Sarge explained.

"Has anybody been ripped off around here?" asked Hawkeye.

Sarge nodded. "Several people. That's why I'm working under cover. I have a full description of this guy, and I'm waiting to see if I can catch him in the act.

"If the heat doesn't get me first," he added, wiping his face with a tattered tissue. "Whew! A little rain would cool things off, but the weatherman says not a chance."

"Sarge, your makeup is coming off," warned Amy, looking at his tissue, which was streaked with brown. "And one of your eyebrows just escaped." She stooped down, picked it up, and handed it back to him.

"Oh, thanks," said Sarge gratefully. He patted the eyebrow back in place over his right eye.

Just then, they heard someone yell, "Stop, thief!"

Hawkeye, Amy, and Sarge looked around. "Over there!" Amy exclaimed, pointing toward West Street. "Come on, hurry!"

She sprinted across Summer Avenue, Hawkeye following close behind. Sarge brought up the rear, puffing and muttering as he ran.

When they got to Grandma's Bakery on West Street, they found a small crowd gathered around a woman who was yelling, "Get the police! Get the police!"

"I'm a policeman, ma'am," Sarge said importantly as he elbowed his way through the crowd. "Stand aside, everybody, stand aside."

"Get away from me, you bum!" screeched the woman, pushing at him.

"Hey, cut it out! I really *am* a policeman," Sarge protested. He fumbled in one of his jacket pockets, brought out his badge, and flashed it in front of her.

"Now, calm down and tell me what happened," he said.

"Someone just stole my camera—snatched it right off my shoulder!" the woman told him.

"What did he look like?" Sarge asked.

"He was young, about medium height, with short hair," she reported. "He was wearing a blue-and-white-striped T-shirt and blue jeans."

Sarge nodded. "That matches the other descriptions I've gotten of this guy," he said to Amy and Hawkeye.

"He was carrying a shopping bag," the woman added. "I grabbed at it to try to stop him and heard it rip."

"A very dangerous thing to do, ma'am," commented Sarge, shaking his head. "You should never try to stop a thief. He might be armed."

"Did you happen to see which way he went?" Hawkeye asked.

"Yes, young man, I did," the woman answered. "He ran up the street, then turned toward the train station."

"I bet you anything he's there now!" said Amy excitedly.

Sarge looked at his watch. "The train to Chicago leaves in eight minutes," he said. "That's probably how he's planning to make his getaway."

"C'mon Sarge," urged Amy. "We have to move fast!"

"Right," agreed Sarge. "Let's go."

They were about to start for the station when Sarge suddenly noticed something lying on the ground. It was a cloth belt.

"Pardon me, ma'am," he said, addressing the woman who had just been robbed. "Did you drop this?"

"It's not mine," the woman replied, shaking her head.

With a shrug, Sarge stuffed the belt into his pants pocket. "OK, let's get going," he said to Hawkeye and Amy.

When they got to the train station, Sarge pointed to a sign next to the door that said, THE AIR CONDITIONING IS BROKEN. WE ARE SORRY FOR THE INCONVENIENCE.

"How do you like that!" Sarge said, puffing hard. "And on the hottest day of the year, too!"

Inside the station, Hawkeye, Amy, and Sarge looked around the small waiting room. Everything seemed normal.

"All I see are five people waiting for the train," Hawkeye finally remarked.

"I'll go check outside," said Sarge. "Maybe our snatcher's hiding somewhere in the area so he can hop the train."

After Sarge left, Hawkeye said to Amy in a low voice, "Let's walk around the waiting room real slowly. Maybe we missed something."

Amy nodded. "Good idea," she replied. "We can pretend we're looking for a friend."

Together they made a circuit of the room. As they walked, they made sure to look at each traveler closely.

Amy pulled Hawkeye back toward the door. "Hawkeye," she whispered, "can you make a sketch of the people without letting them see you do it? I think it might give us a clue."

"No sweat," Hawkeye whispered back.

He slowly pulled his sketch pad and pencil out of his back pocket. Leaning against the wall and trying to look as casual as possible, he started to draw the travelers.

When he had finished drawing, he looked carefully at the completed sketch. Then his jaw dropped in amazement.

"Oh, wow, Amy!" he whispered. "Do you see what I see?"

Trying to look casual about it, Hawkeye drew the travelers in the waiting room.

Amy peered over his shoulder and studied the sketch. Then she nodded excitedly. "We'd better show this to Sarge fast—before the train comes!"

WHAT CONVINCED HAWKEYE AND AMY THAT THEY HAD SPOTTED THE THIEF?

See page 91

SOLUTIONS

The Case of the Bragging Boyfriend

Hawkeye remembered Pete saying he had lost one of his sneakers during the climb. No one in his right mind would wear sneakers while climbing to the top of a snowy mountain. Besides, in the photo, Pete was wearing hiking boots.

"Not only that," Hawkeye added. "Pete claimed he got to the top in three hours. It takes days to climb Mount Everest—it's the highest mountain in the world.

"I don't know if Pete's other stories are true or not," he told Laurel, "but I wouldn't count on it!"

Laurel didn't wait to find out. She simply told Pete to take a hike!

69

The Case of the Splattered Sheets

Hawkeye's sketch revealed half of the line trailing along the ground. The sheets were still fastened to the line by clothespins. If a big dog like Nosey had pulled the sheets down, they would have snapped right out of the clothespins.

"And look at Nosey's paw prints," said Hawkeye. "They come in a straight line across the yard and the sheets, which means the sheets must have already been on the ground when Nosey ran through here."

"But there are some other footprints under the sheets and around the clothesline pole," Amy said angrily. "I bet they belong to Macho, and I bet he unhooked the clothesline!"

"Right," Hawkeye agreed. "But we don't have any proof. The best we can do is prove to Mrs. Ratchet that Nosey isn't guilty."

They left the sketch inside her mailbox along with a written explanation of the facts. Mrs. Ratchet called Hawkeye to apologize. Then she warned him to keep Nosey away from her yard in the future—or else!

The Mystery of the Telltale Timepiece

Besides the computer monitor and keyboard, Hawkeye's sketch of the items in the window also revealed a digital wristwatch, a radio, some speakers, and an unplugged electric clock. The wristwatch showed the correct time—11:05. The electric clock read 4:40.

As Hawkeye explained, "Since Mr. Traynor said that his clocks and watches were always accurate, the electric clock must have been accidentally unplugged by the thief—and stopped at the time of the crime. After we knew when the crime took place, we also knew which suspect might be lying—Mike Graham. Mike couldn't account for his whereabouts before five-thirty and could have been lying when he said he was in bed asleep until five o'clock. But Josh could prove he was fishing during the time the crime was committed."

"Not only that," Amy added triumphantly, "but the watch Josh was looking at was still in the window. If he'd been the thief, that would have been the first thing he'd have taken."

Later that day, when confronted with the

continued

73

facts of the case, Mike Graham broke down and confessed to the robbery.

Sarge was so pleased with Hawkeye and Amy's speedy wrap-up of the case that he treated them and Mr. Traynor to lunch at the Eatery.

The Case of the Computer Cutup

When Amy looked at the message closely, she realized that she was looking at a word rebus. In this kind of puzzle, words and parts of words are added and/or subtracted to get a message.

But when Amy solved the rebus, what she got was a name—Corey Callahan. She remembered that Corey had said he liked crazy jokes, puzzles, mysteries—and especially computers. So it made perfect sense to Amy that Corey would leave a humorous message in the form of a puzzle on a computer screen.

"It's easy," Amy explained to Mike and Sally. "BACK – BAK + DOOR – DO + EYE – E. That leaves C, OR, and EY—Corey. Then C + ALLOW – OW – AHA + SNAIL – SAIL. That leaves C, ALL, AHA, N—Callahan."

"Okay, but what about the 'Chomp Chomp How About Another Byte, part?" Mike asked.

"That stumped me at first," Amy admitted. "But then I figured it out. Corey's new here, right? Well, he likes computers so much, he probably wants to join the Bytes. And this

continued

77

is how he decided to ask us if he can become a member!"

The next afternoon when Hawkeye and Amy went over to Corey's house, Amy told him what she'd found. Corey admitted he'd sneaked into the computer room before class, hid Mike's disk, and programmed another disk with his message. Then he labeled the new disk with the name of Mike's program. He apologized and promised to return Mike's disk. He also said he hoped they'd still let him join the computer club. (They did!)

The Secret of the Loon Lake Monster

Amy noticed shadows in Mr. Babbit's photo and realized the picture was a fake. A few minutes earlier, she and Hawkeye had had to squint into the afternoon sun when they looked out across the water. In Mr. Babbit's snapshot, which he said he took in the afternoon, the sun was shining from behind him, and the shadow of the pier pointed toward the middle of the lake. The shadow that Loonie supposedly cast, however, pointed in the opposite direction.

"The picture is a fake," admitted an embarrassed Mr. Babbit. "I have seen Loonie myself, and I just thought a photograph of it would make people want to visit Loon Lake. I'll—I'll tell the newspapers the truth."

Hawkeye suddenly grabbed Amy's arm.

"Look!" he said. "What's that?"

Amy peered into the distance. "It's your imagination, Hawkeye. I'm looking as hard as I can, and I don't see anything except logs."

Amy grinned at him. "Of course, you never can tell. Loonie may turn out to be shaped just like a log!"

READ THE SOLUTIONS IN YOUR MIRROR

The Case of the Nabbed Necklace

Something about Joe's story didn't make sense to Hawkeye. And when Amy saw the sketch, she knew exactly what Hawkeye was talking about!

The sketch showed the guard's desk. There was a crossword puzzle on top, and near the puzzle was a fountain pen, not a pencil. The guard said he had been erasing a wrong answer when the lights went out. But ink can't be erased easily, and besides, no eraser was visible.

Hawkeye and Amy suspected that the guard had made up the whole story, and that he was probably the thief.

Their suspicions proved true. When the lights went out, the guard had sneaked up to the display case and grabbed the necklace.

"I don't know how to thank you two," Mr. Bagley told Hawkeye and Amy later that afternoon. " 'Joe' is actually a jewel thief named Rudolf Carstairs. He replaced the real special guard before the necklace arrived in Lakewood Hills."

"That explains why he didn't answer to

continued

his name right away when we found him at the desk," said Hawkeye.

Amy grinned. "Well, whatever his name is, he should feel right at home where he's going—he'll have plenty of guards around him and lots of time to do crossword puzzles!"

The Secret of the Concealed Cash

When Hawkeye looked at his list, he noticed that all the books were neatly arranged in alphabetical order, by author. However, one book was out of order—Selected Poems by Emily Dickinson.

"Here it is!" Hawkeye exclaimed dramatically as he pulled the Dickinson book from the shelf. Hoping that his hunch was right, he slowly riffled the pages of the book.

Mrs. von Buttermore gasped when the envelope containing the money appeared between pages 100 and 101. "Please forgive me for doubting your word, Hawkeye," she said. "You were absolutely right!"

After Henry discovered that Maggie had left the house, bag and baggage, Mrs. von Buttermore had him call the police. Then she told him to prepare an extraspecial lunch for Hawkeye and Amy—the best detectives in the whole state!

The Mystery of the Midnight Trickster

When Paul was more awake, Hawkeye showed him the sketch and explained how he had figured out who the trickster might be. "While I was drawing," I noticed that Tommy Spano had gone to bed with his sneakers on.

"But later," Hawkeye continued, "when Keith sent everybody back to bed, Tommy stubbed his bare toe on a tent stake.

"What really convinced me, though," he went on, "was when I looked at my sketch again, then looked at Tommy's tent. His sneakers were still sticking out of his tent—and they were on the wrong feet!"

Hawkeye took Tommy aside and told him what he had deduced.

Tommy admitted he had played all those tricks, always setting up his sneakers to make it look as if he were in his tent. He confessed that he hated camping and he had hoped his pranks would get everybody sent home.

Tommy apologized to everyone that night after dinner and promised that his trick-playing days were over.

The Case of the Camera Snatcher

Amy and Hawkeye noticed that four of the travelers in the waiting room were dressed for the weather. The fifth traveler was wearing a trench coat. It seemed ridiculous that anyone would wear a heavy raincoat in a heat wave with no chance of rain—unless he had something to hide.

"Another thing tipped me off, too," Amy explained later, after Sarge had made his arrest, and discovered half a dozen gold chains and the woman's camera in the thief's pockets. "His raincoat belt was missing! There were empty loops where the belt should've been.

"I figured that the belt Sarge picked up at the scene of the crime must have belonged to him. It probably fell out of his shopping bag when the lady ripped it."

"And speaking of the shopping bag," Hawkeye added, "it was sticking out of a trash can next to one of the chairs."

Sarge, who by now had changed back into his uniform, looked at Hawkeye and Amy gratefully.

continued

"Hey, this calls for a celebration," he said. "How about getting some ice cream? My treat!"

Hawkeye and Amy thought that was a great idea, and for the rest of the afternoon, they sat in the ice cream shop and celebrated with Banana Bombshells.

Dear Friend:

Would you like to become a member of the Can You Solve the Mystery?™ Reading Panel? It's easy to do. After you've read this book, find a piece of paper. Then answer the questions you see below on your piece of paper (be sure to number the answers). Please don't write in the book. Mail your answer sheet to:

Meadowbrook Books
Dept. CYSI-L
18318 Minnetonka Blvd.
Deephaven, MN 55391

Thanks a lot for your replies—they really help us!

1. How old are you?
2. What is your first and last name?
3. What is your address?
4. What grade are you in this year?
5. Are you a boy or a girl?
6. Where did you get this book? (Read all answers first. Then choose the one that you like best and write the letter on your paper.)

6A. Gift
6B. Bookstore
6C. Other store
6D. School library

6E. Public library
6F. Borrowed from a friend
6G. Other (What?)

7. If you chose the book yourself, why did you choose it? (Be sure you read all the answers listed first. Then choose the one that you like best and write the letter on your paper.)

7A. I like to read mysteries.
7B. The cover looked interesting.
7C. The title sounded good.
7D. I like to solve mysteries.
7E. A librarian suggested it.
7F. A teacher suggested it.
7G. A friend liked it.
7H. The picture clues looked interesting.
7I. Hawkeye and Amy looked interesting.
7J. Other (What?)

8. How did you like the book? (Write your letter choice on your paper.)

  8A. Liked a lot   8B. Liked   8C. Not sure
      8D. Disliked   8E. Disliked a lot

9. How did you like the picture clues? (Write your letter choice on your paper.)

  9A. Liked a lot   9B. Liked   9C. Not sure
      9D. Disliked   9E. Disliked a lot

10. What story did you like best? Why?

11. What story did you like least? Why?

12. Would you like to read more stories about Hawkeye and Amy?

13. Would you like to read more stories about Hawkeye alone?

14. Would you like to read more stories about Amy alone?

15. Which would you prefer? (Be sure to read all the answers first. Then choose the one you like best and write the letter on your paper.)

  15A. One long story with lots of picture clues.
  15B. One long story with only one picture clue at the end.
  15C. One long story with no picture clues at all.
  15D. A CAN YOU SOLVE THE MYSTERY?™ video game
  15E. A CAN YOU SOLVE THE MYSTERY?™ comic strip.
  15F. A CAN YOU SOLVE THE MYSTERY?™ comic book.

16. Who was your favorite person in the book? Why?

17. How hard were the mysteries to solve? (Write your letter choice on your paper.)

  17A. Too easy   17B. A little easy   17C. Just right
      17D. A little hard   17E. Too hard

18. How hard was the book to read and understand? (Write your letter choice on your paper.)

    18A. Too easy   18B. A little easy   18C. Just right
        18D. A little hard   18E. Too hard

19. Have you read any other CAN YOU SOLVE THE MYSTERY?™ books? How many? What were the titles of the books?

20. What other books do you like to read? (You can write in books that aren't mysteries, too.)

21. Would you buy another volume of this mystery series?

22. Do you have any suggestions or comments about the book? What are they?

23. What is the volume number on this book? (Look on the front cover.)

24. Do you have a computer at home?

HAVE YOU SOLVED ALL OF THESE EXCITING CASES?

Volume #1

THE SECRET OF THE LONG-LOST COUSIN

Only $2.75 ppd.
ISBN 0-915658-81-X

A stranger arrives at Hawkeye's house from Alaska, claiming he's a cousin of Hawkeye's mother. But something bothers Hawkeye. So in the middle of the night, he creeps to the living room to study an old family photo. His sharp eyes pick up important clues... plus nine other mysteries!

HOW DOES HAWKEYE DECIDE WHETHER THE STRANGER IS A REAL COUSIN OR A PHONY?

Volume #2

THE CASE OF THE CHOCOLATE SNATCHER

Only $2.75 ppd.
ISBN 0-915658-85-2

A drugstore clerk reports that a masked thief has just stolen a small fortune in fancy chocolates. The getaway car leads Hawkeye, Amy, and Sergeant Treadwell to three suspects. Each of them has a perfect alibi, but Hawkeye makes a lightning-fast sketch and cracks the case... plus eight other mysteries!

HOW DID HAWKEYE KNOW WHICH SUSPECT WAS LYING?

Volume #3

THE CASE OF THE VIDEO GAME SMUGGLERS

Only $2.75 ppd.
ISBN 0-915658-88-7

Hawkeye, Amy and Sergeant Treadwell must catch the crooks who stole the video game their computer club just invented. At the airport scanner gate, Hawkeye sketches suspects who could be smuggling the disk. With seconds to spare, he and Amy pick out the thieves... plus nine other mysteries!

WHOM DOES HAWKEYE SPOT AS THE SMUGGLER, AND WHERE IS THE COMPUTER DISK HIDDEN?

Volume #4

THE CASE OF THE MYSTERIOUS DOGNAPPER

Only $2.75 ppd.
ISBN 0-915658-95-X

While Hawkeye and Amy are visiting Mrs. von Buttermore at her mansion, her Great Dane, Priceless, is stolen. Several people could be the dognapper, but Hawkeye and Amy take one look at the ransom note that arrives and immediately figure out who's guilty... plus nine other mysteries!

HOW DO HAWKEYE AND AMY KNOW WHO TOOK PRICELESS?

Collect all of Hawkeye's and Amy's cases—and solve 'em yourself!

Volume #5

THE CASE OF THE CLEVER COMPUTER CROOKS

Only $2.75 ppd.
ISBN 0-915658-11-9

Hawkeye and Amy must find out how someone stole hundreds of computers from a warehouse. The video camera in the warehouse was working the whole time, but the film from the camera shows the strangest thing—one minute there are hundreds of computers in the room and the next minute the room is empty. Hawkeye does a sketch of the warehouse and realizes how the crooks did it . . . plus eight other mysteries!

HOW DID THE CROOKS STEAL THE COMPUTERS?

Volume #6

THE CASE OF THE FAMOUS CHOCOLATE CHIP COOKIES

Only $2.75 ppd.
ISBN 0-915658-15-1

Grandma Johnson's cookie recipe is gone. Whoever stole it left a clue in the Cookie Works. Sergeant Treadwell needs the help of Amy and Hawkeye to crack this case. They find the thief with just a few clues. Can you? . . . plus eight other mysteries!

HOW DOES HAWKEYE SPOT THE RECIPE ROBBER FROM CLUES IN GRANDMA JOHNSON'S OFFICE?

Volume #7

THE MYSTERY OF THE "STAR SHIP" MOVIE

Only $2.75 ppd.
ISBN 0-915658-20-8

Amy and Hawkeye are visiting the set of their favorite movie, "Star Ship." Suddenly a man runs past them with a stolen copy of the film and the mystery begins. The thief is hiding somewhere on a set filled with robots and space ships. Amy uses Hawkeye's drawing to figure out who stole the film. Can you? . . . plus eight other mysteries!

HOW DOES AMY FIND THE THIEF HIDING AMONG THE ROBOT REPAIRMEN?

Volume #8

THE SECRET OF THE SOFTWARE SPY

Only $2.75 ppd.
ISBN 0-915658-25-9

Sergeant Treadwell knows that the spy who stole some computer software is going to eat at a fancy French restaurant. Amy and Hawkeye need to find the spy among the diners in a crowded restaurant. Hawkeye locates the prime suspect with only a few clues to go on . . . plus eight other mysteries!

HOW DOES HAWKEYE SINGLE OUT THE SOFTWARE SPY IN A CROWDED RESTAURANT

Collect all of Hawkeye's and Amy's cases—and solve 'em yourself!

FREE STUFF FOR KIDS

The latest edition has even more fun playthings than ever before! Over 250 of the best free and up-to-a-dollar things kids can get by mail:

- a sample of Mount St. Helen's ash
- a tiny blue spruce tree
- the Louisville-Slugger-Bat key chain
- Wizard of Oz stationery
- a strawberry plant
- a compass and booklet on orienteering
- and much more

Only $3.75 ppd.

Our Pledge: the suppliers have promised in writing to honor single copy requests. We monitor the suppliers and keep this book up-to-date and accurate.

ORDER FORM

Name _____

Address _____

City _____ State _____ Zip _____

Please charge my _____ Visa _____ Mastercharge Account

Acct. # _____ Exp. Date _____

Signature _____

Check or money order payable to Meadowbrook Press.

Quant.	Title	Cost Per Book	Amount
	#1 The Secret of the Long-Lost Cousin	$2.75	
	#2 The Case of the Chocolate Snatcher	$2.75	
	#3 The Case of the Video Game Smugglers	$2.75	
	#4 The Case of the Mysterious Dognappers	$2.75	
	#5 The Case of the Famous Chocolate Chip Cookies	$2.75	
	#6 The Mystery of the Star Ship Movie	$2.75	
	#7 The Secret of the Software Spy	$2.75	
	#8 The Case of the Clever Computer Crooks	$2.75	
	#9 The Case of the Toilet Paper Decorator	$2.75	
	#10 The Secret of the Loon Lake Monster	$2.75	
	Free Stuff for Kids	$3.75	
	TOTAL		

We do not ship C.O.D. Postage and handling is included in all prices. Your group or organization may qualify for group quantity discounts: please write for further information to Direct Mail Dept., Meadowbrook Press, 18318 Minnetonka Blvd., Deephaven, MN 55391.

Meadowbrook

18318 Minnetonka Boulevard • Deephaven, MN 55391 • (612) 473-5400